ROBIN TO THE RESCUE!

Adapted by TRACEY WEST

Based on the screenplay by
Seth Grahame-Smith and
Chris McKenna & Erik Sommers,
with additional material
by Jared Stern & John Whittington,
based on LEGO Construction Toys.

Scholastic Ltd

Scholastic Children's Books
Euston House,
24 Eversholt Street,
London NW1 1DB, UK

A division of Scholastic Ltd
London ~ New York ~ Toronto ~ Sydney ~ Auckland
Mexico City ~ New Delhi ~ Hong Kong

This book was first published in the US by Scholastic Inc, 2017, as two titles:
Robin to the Rescue
I'm Batgirl
This edition published in the UK by Scholastic Ltd, 2017

ISBN 978 1407 18119 6

Based on the story by Seth Grahame-Smith and the screenplay by Seth
Grahame-Smith and Chris McKenna & Erik Sommers and Jared Stern & John
Whittington.

Printed in Slovakia by TBB

2 4 6 8 10 9 7 5 3 1

Papers used by Scholastic Children's Books are made from wood grown in
sustainable forests.

www.scholastic.co.uk

FSC
www.fsc.org

MIX
From responsible
sources
FSC® C022120

Hi, I'm Dick Grayson. Not too long ago, I was lonely. I had no family. I dreamed of being part of a family again someday.

Then one night my dream came true! Let me tell you how it happened.

My story begins in Gotham City Orphanage.
Lots of kids live there. It was hard to feel special.
I knew I had to stand out if I wanted to be adopted,
so I worked on my skills. I wanted to be the best
Dick Grayson I could be.

Two heroes inspired me. First, there was Batman, the ultimate Super Hero. He kept Gotham City safe from crime. Next, there was Bruce Wayne, the ultimate orphan. He had no family, just like me, but he was very successful, lived in a big mansion and rode around in a limo.

BATMAN

BRUCE WAYNE

One day, I was outside the orphanage when Batman drove past! I couldn't believe it.

"No way! Look who's here!" I yelled.

The other kids ran towards the Batmobile. They bumped into me and pushed me. I couldn't get close!

"The Speedwagon"

"Hey, kids, who wants a shot from the merch gun?" Batman yelled.

Everyone cheered. He shot cool Batman-themed toys into the crowd. But I didn't get anything.

I watched, empty-handed, as my hero drove away.

I didn't let it get me down, though. And that night, I got lucky!

There was a big party for Police Commissioner Jim Gordon. He was retiring. The orphan choir was there to sing for the crowd, and I was part of the group.

I was singing when I spotted my other hero – Bruce Wayne!

I ran up to him and he took a selfie with me.

"Whoa! Thanks, Mr Wayne," I said.

"Call me Bruce, champ," he told me.

"I'm just so happy to meet you, sir," I said. "And I have a question for you. Do you want to adopt a child?"

Mr Wayne wasn't looking at me, and he seemed a little distracted. But he answered, "Yeah."

Excellent news!

"One with upgraded features like cooking, or driftwood art or street magic?" I asked.

"Sure, that all sounds great," Bruce said as he signed another autograph.

"Do you think you would be interested in adopting me, Mr Wayne?" I asked.

"A million per cent," Mr Wayne said, looking at the stage where the ceremony was starting.

"This is great!" I said. "Because all I want to do is get adopted so I can stop being..."

Mr Wayne walked away before I could finish my sentence.

"... alone."

I know that Mr Wayne walked away from me. But I didn't let it get me down. After all, he *did* say that he would adopt me!

I wasn't going to let my chance to get adopted slip by. So I went outside and looked for Mr Wayne's butler, Alfred.

Alfred believed me. He let me ride in the Wayne limo. That was swell!

I think Alfred helped me because he knew that deep down, Bruce Wayne missed his family. He wanted Bruce to have a family again.

Alfred drove me to Wayne Manor. It was the fanciest place I had ever seen. And now it was my home!

I ran through the hallways, exploring every room. When I went into the library, something amazing happened.

I touched a bookcase and the whole thing swung open. There was a fireman's pole behind it! I slid down the pole. When I landed, I was in an underground headquarters.

I looked around. I saw Batman's vehicles and Batman's crime-fighting tools. That's when it hit me.

I was inside the Batcave!

SECURITY CAM 023
AUTO TRACKING ON OFF
FD 35.2987
50mm
10:48:30 AM
00:21:12:16
PLAY
ZOOM F

"Don't touch that," a voice said, and I turned around. Batman was there!

I couldn't believe it! "Batman lives in Bruce Wayne's basement?!" I asked.

Batman was surprised to see me. "No, Bruce Wayne lives in Batman's attic," he said.

Batman was busy on his computer trying to figure out a problem: how to put the Joker into the Phantom Zone. That's the place that holds the baddest, meanest villains of all time.

"*The Joker can only be put in the Phantom Zone using the Phantom Zone Projector,*" the computer told him. "*The projector is deep inside Superman's Fortress of Solitude, inside a cauldron. Only an object seven centimetres in diameter can fit inside the cauldron.*"

"I can't fit in there. I am way too buff," Batman said. Then he looked at me. "Hey, kid!"

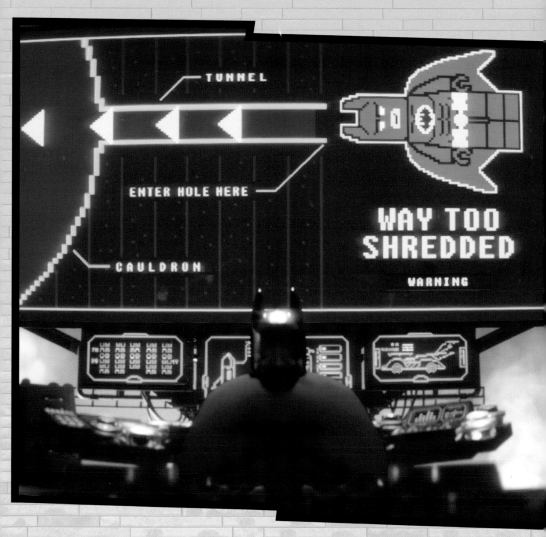

"You're nimble, right?" he asked me.

"Yes," I said.

"And small?" he asked.

"Very!" I said.

"And quiet?" he asked.

"When I desire to be," I whispered.

"Great!" Batman said. "Follow me."
Then Batman walked into a room with all his costumes and gear. "Preparing mission gear," the Batcave computer said. I couldn't believe my eyes!

"Do I get a costume, too?" I asked.

Seeing all the costumes got me excited. I didn't wait for Batman to answer. I started trying them on. The computer named them as I wore them.

The Mariachi. Glam Bat. Clawed Rain.

"No, no and ... no," Batman said.

Then I spotted a cool costume called "Reggae Man". It had a red shirt with green sleeves. Red boots. A yellow cape. And green trousers. The trousers were kind of tight, so I ripped them off. Luckily I was wearing green shorts.

"Now I'm free, now I'm moving. Come on, Batman, let's get grooving!" I rhymed.

We were about to leave when I realized something. I needed permission from my new dad, Bruce Wayne, to leave the mansion.

"Well, Bruce and I decided to share custody of you," Batman said. "So you are mission approved!"

"Woo-hoo!" I cheered. "A month ago I had no dads, then I had one dad, now I have two dads and one of them is Batman!"

I jumped into the Batmobile. Then it hit me. I was in the Batmobile. Next to Batman. Wearing a costume.

I was a Super Hero sidekick!

"So are you ready to follow Batman and learn a few life lessons along the way?" Batman asked.

"I sure am, Dad Two!" I answered.

Then we sped out of the Batcave, into the night.

We zoomed down the road. Then wings popped out of the Batmobile and it started to fly! We soared across the night sky and flew to Superman's Fortress of Solitude. It looked like a castle made of ice.

"Superman has zero friends," Batman told me. "So I'll keep him busy while you sneak into that air vent and get the projector, got it?"

I nodded. I think Batman was a little bit jealous of Superman, and they didn't always get along very well. I couldn't wait to show Batman all my skills. I crawled through the vent to get to the cauldron that held the projector.

Batman rang the doorbell and Superman answered. He wasn't alone. Through the vent, I could see a big party going on inside. Everyone in the Justice League was there. Batman spotted Wonder Woman, The Flash, Green Lantern, Aquaman and many more.

"Are you really having this party without me?" Batman asked.

The Justice League members all looked away from Batman. It was pretty awkward!

"Um, I guess there must have been a mistake with the email," Superman answered.

I felt bad for my new Batman Dad. I think it hurt his feelings that he wasn't invited, and maybe he realized he should work on his teamwork skills. But we were on a mission. And it was good that the place was so crowded.

I reached a tunnel leading to the Phantom Zone Projector, but it was blocked by lasers. Batman sneaked away to help me and nobody even noticed.

Batman fixed it so the lasers went dead.
"Now do everything I say. Jump!" he instructed.
"Okay!" I said.
Batman and I worked as a team as I flipped, dodged and somersaulted my way through the razor-sharp claws of the Jaws of Death.

After that, I had to leap through rings of fire without getting burnt.

Finally, I reached the cauldron and found the Phantom Zone Projector! I grabbed it and met Batman outside.

"Here you go, Dad!" I said. "How did I do?"

"Watching you ... out there ... it made me feel so proud."

"Oh, you're such a great dad," I said. I started to hug him.

"What are you doing?" asked Batman.

"Trying to give you a big old hug," I replied.

Batman seemed a little uncomfortable, but I think that deep down he was happy we were such a good team.

We jumped into the Batwing, and I felt really happy. My days of being lonely were over.

Now I had a family and I was a Super Hero sidekick, too. And I couldn't wait to have more adventures with Batman!

We still had bad guys to fight. And Robin to save. And the Joker to catch. But from that moment on, I was part of Batman's team.

I was Batgirl!

I'M BATGIRL!

Adapted by TRACEY WEST

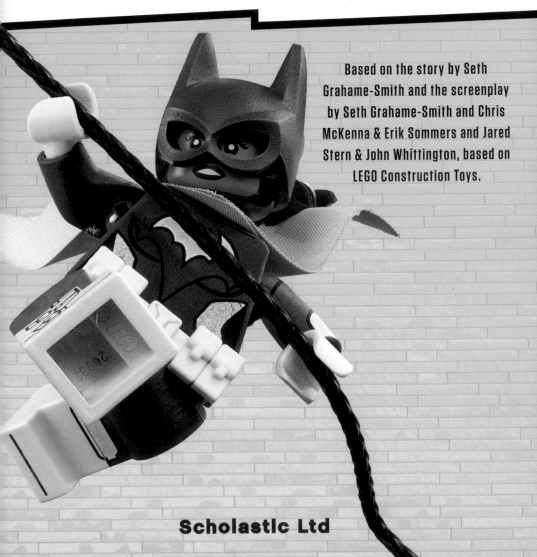

Based on the story by Seth Grahame-Smith and the screenplay by Seth Grahame-Smith and Chris McKenna & Erik Sommers and Jared Stern & John Whittington, based on LEGO Construction Toys.

Scholastic Ltd

Scholastic Children's Books
Euston House,
24 Eversholt Street,
London NW1 1DB, UK

A division of Scholastic Ltd
London ~ New York ~ Toronto ~ Sydney ~ Auckland
Mexico City ~ New Delhi ~ Hong Kong

This book was first published in the US by Scholastic Inc, 2017, as two titles:
Robin to the Rescue
I'm Batgirl
This edition published in the UK by Scholastic Ltd, 2017

ISBN 978 1407 18119 6

Based on the story by Seth Grahame-Smith and the screenplay by Seth
Grahame-Smith and Chris McKenna & Erik Sommers and Jared Stern & John
Whittington.

Printed in Slovakia by TBB

2 4 6 8 10 9 7 5 3 1

Papers used by Scholastic Children's Books are made from wood grown
in sustainable forests.

www.scholastic.co.uk

My name is Barbara Gordon. I'm the police commissioner of Gotham City. You might say I was born for the job. My dad, Jim Gordon, was commissioner for a long time.

My dad had help watching over Gotham City. Batman was always on call when he needed him. All my dad had to do was turn on the Bat-Signal.

But I looked up to my dad most of all. Growing up, I knew I wanted to be a police officer, just like him.

I was top of my class at Harvard for Police. Then I got a job in the town of Blüdhaven. I cleaned up the streets there. And I didn't need Batman to do it. Instead, I worked with my excellent team of police officers.

Then my dad retired. Gotham City offered me the job of police commissioner. My childhood dream had come true! I wanted the job. But I wasn't sure about one thing: Batman. I liked working on a team, and Batman wasn't exactly a team player.

The city held a big party for my dad's retirement.

That night, at the party, I gave a speech.

"Look, Batman's been on the job for a very, very, very, very long time," I said. "However, in spite of having a full-time Batman, Gotham City is still the most crime-ridden city in the world."

People in the crowd started to mumble. I knew they agreed with me. But billionaire Bruce Wayne argued with me.

"What's your problem with Batman?" he asked. "What did Batman do to you?"

"I'm not a Batman hater," I replied. "But we don't need an unsupervised, adult man in a Halloween costume karate-chopping our citizens left, right and centre. What I want is to partner with Batman."

"No!" Bruce exclaimed.

"Wouldn't that be better?" I asked. "I'm sure Batman could use the help."

I was about to finish my speech when a load of ice cream vans pulled up all around the gala. The doors opened and bad guys started pouring out. I knew those clowns were trouble.

"Everybody get down!" I yelled.

    The Joker showed up, followed by the rest of Gotham City's super-villains.

    I ran towards the Joker, ready to face him. But who do you think came between us? You guessed it. Batman!

"Oh, Batman's here!" the Joker said. "Wonderful! I've got a surprise for you guys, and it's going to make you smile. I ... surrender!"

I was surprised. So was Batman. Even the super-villains looked surprised.

But it was no joke. The Joker calmly climbed into the back of a police car.

"Joker, you have the right to remain silent," I told him.

"Okay!" said the Joker cheerfully.

But Batman was suspicious of the Joker. He looked at me.

"And you have the right to chill out for one second because the Joker is not surrendering to you!" he insisted.

"We can question him together, okay?" I asked.
But that wasn't okay with Batman. "Look, the
Joker wants to go to Arkham Asylum," he said.
"That's the last place *any* criminal wants to go.
Unless – *ding ding ding!* – he's got some big plan."
"What if you put him in the Phantom Zone?"
somebody in the crowd called out.

"The Phantom Zone! That's a great idea," Batman said.

He tried to pull the Joker out of the police car, but I had my officers stop him. Once again, Batman was trying to do things by himself. And we needed to work together.

We rounded up all the super-villains and locked them in Arkham Asylum with the Joker. All but one. I noticed that Harley Quinn was missing. So I called Batman to let him know. I hoped we could work together to find her.

But Batman wasn't interested in working together. He showed up at Arkham Asylum with some kid in a costume and a Phantom Zone Projector. Then he blasted the Joker into the Phantom Zone!

I was tired of Batman taking things into his own
hands. I locked him in a cell.

We quickly learned that Batman was right. The
Joker's surrender was a trap – just not the trap
Batman expected. Harley Quinn grabbed the
Phantom Zone Projector and used it to open up
the Phantom Zone.

The Phantom Zone hovered above the city. Then the Joker's face appeared all over Gotham City.

"I could never take over the city with all the old loser villains," the Joker said. "So I've collected some new Gotham City friends to help out!"

The Joker and his new evil friends started causing trouble right away! I knew I needed Batman's help with this. But I really needed him to work as a team this time.

"I don't need anyone's help," Batman said firmly.

I wanted to leave Batman in his cell when he said that.

But there was a kid there, along with Bruce Wayne's butler, Alfred. The kid convinced Batman to help us.

I let him out of prison. "But you have to promise you'll team up with me until the end," I warned him.

"I promise," Batman said. "I'll do whatever it takes to stop the Joker. Even if it means working as a team. Let's go!"

"Now, Barbara, you are officially representing the Batman brand," he told me. "That means you have to use officially licensed gadgets."

Batman started shooting stuff out of his merch gun.

Kaboom! He shot out a costume for Alfred.

He shot out a bunch of Bat-gadgets for the kid and me, too.

Now we were a real crime-fighting team!

We left Arkham Asylum. The Joker and his evil friends had taken over the streets of Gotham City. I tried to lead the team to safety.

"Okay, follow me," I told the others. "Batman, you're my cover. Robin, Alfred, you're lookouts."

But Batman didn't follow me. He ran right past me!

"Batman, what are you doing?" I asked.

"I'm following ahead of you," he replied.

"The phrase is following *behind* you," I said.

I quickly figured out that Batman was lying when he said he wanted to work as a team. All my cool Bat-gadgets were made of chocolate, useless against the bad guys. But he wouldn't share his tools.

And when he built us a Batwing, it only had room for one! We had to cram in there.

Scary bad guys were taking over the city! Batman had no choice. He had to let us help him. Together, Batman, Alfred, Robin and I took down some big baddies.

But we still needed to capture the Joker. Batman wanted to do it all by himself. So he locked me, Alfred and Robin into the Batwing.

He left us, and the Joker's evil friends attacked the Batwing. Robin escaped and ran to find Batman. Then Alfred and I escaped. But the bad guys captured Robin!

That's when Batman showed up.

I was angry with Batman. I started to walk away.
"Barbara, please don't leave," he said.
I stopped. "Why?" I asked.
"Because there's something I need to say to you,"
he replied. "Click."

I frowned. "Click? Click doesn't mean anything, Batman," I said.

"Sorry, you've got to turn around," Batman told me.

I turned around. The Bat-Signal flashed in the night sky. But it was different.

It looked like me.

"I call it the Babs-signal," Batman said. "And I'm flipping the switch for you because I really need your help, Barbara. I really, really do. What do you say, Commissioner? Will you work with me?"

I shook his hand. "Always," I said.